S0-ARK-538

© 1996 Jim Henson Productions, Inc. MUPPET PRESS, MUPPETS, MUPPET KIDS, and character names and likenesses are trademarks of Jim Henson Productions, Inc. All rights reserved, including the right to reproduce this book or portions thereof in any form. VALUES TO GROW ON is a trademark of Grolier Inc.
Grolier Books is a Division of Grolier Enterprises, Inc.

Printed in the U.S.A.


ISBN 0-7172-8705-X

# JIM HENSON'S MUPPETS

IN

# Bean Makes the Best of It

## A Book About Appreciation

**By Bonnie Worth** • **Illustrated by Joe Ewers**

## GROLIER
B O O K S

Today was Bean's first day at Camp Wocka-Wocka. He hopped onto the bus and sat down next to Kermit.

"Hey," said Kermit, "neat backpack!"

"Thanks," said Bean proudly. "My brother Benny took it to the Grand Canyon."

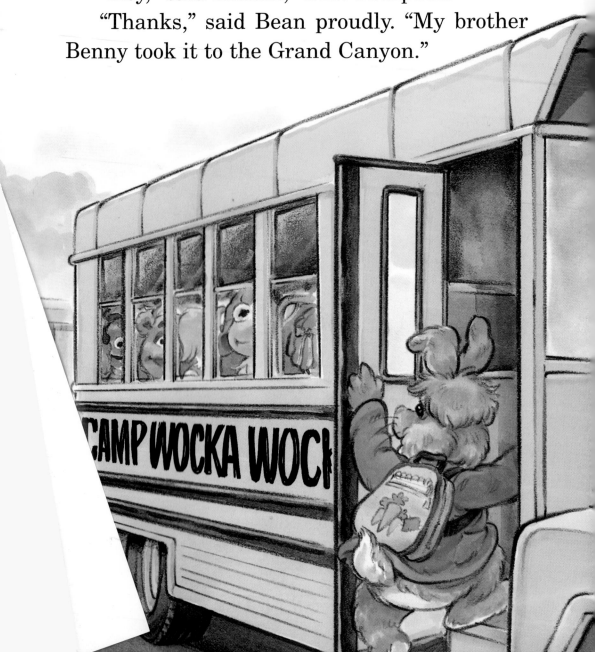

Just last night Bean's mother had dug it out from the hand-me-down closet. Because Bean had so many brothers and sisters, almost everything he owned came from that closet.

"My backpack's from L.L. Jelly Bean," Kermit said excitedly. Then he showed Bean all the special pockets for tools and his bird-viewer.

"Look!" said Fozzie. "My backpack has jokes on the flaps. Listen to this one: Why did the chicken hike over the mountain?" He lifted the flap. "To get to the other camp!"

Bean tried to smile. The only thing his backpack had was a sewn-on patch to keep his pens from falling out.

Soon all of the kids were showing off their new backpacks. Rowlf's had a music chip. Skeeter's had water-bottle holders. Piggy's was designer.

Bean Bunny wished his backpack had been left at the Grand Canyon. Then he could have had a new one, too.

That morning the camp counselor, Ms. Halen-Hearty, led the campers on a nature walk. When she pointed to a red-tufted woodpecker, everyone oohed and ahhed. Everyone except Bean Bunny.

"What's the problem, Bean?" Ms. Halen-Hearty asked later.

Bean sighed. "The other kids have new back-packs. Mine is just an old hand-me-down."

Ms. Halen-Hearty showed Bean her back-pack. "I've had mine for years," she said. "See?"

Bean looked inside. It was crammed with all kinds of interesting odds and ends. "It sure holds a lot," he said.

"And it keeps everything dry," added Ms. Halen-Hearty. "Fancy things are nice, Bean, but all you really need are the basics."

Later, during rest hour, the kids were in their lean-to playing quietly. Fozzie was reading a book of camp jokes. Rowlf was listening to his Squawkman. Piggy was playing cat's cradle with Kermit. And Bean was writing nature notes in his notebook.

Bean was feeling much better. What Ms. Halen-Hearty had said about the basics made sense to him. Then he noticed Scooter writing nature notes, too. Only Scooter was writing them on his laptop computer! Bean looked at his own notebook. It sure was basic. Basically boring!

The next morning Ms. Halen-Hearty said, "Bean, let's have a look at your nature notebook."

"Okay, but it's basically boring," he warned her. "Scooter's is much better."

Ms. Halen-Hearty looked over his notes. "Bean," she said, "a computer is a tool, just like a pen is a tool. You don't need a fancy computer to write well. All you need are the basics."

After that, Bean felt a little better.

That night when Bean got home, he looked in the hand-me-down closet. He found a tom-tom to take to music circle the next day. Bean was fluffing up its frayed feathers when Piggy called.

"I'm bringing a shiny new kazoo to music circle," she said. "And Rowlf is bringing a real synthesizer! What are you bringing, Bean?"

"A tom-tom," Bean murmured.

"Oh, you mean the one your sister Bonnie used in the school play last year? How sweet!" said Piggy.

Bean hung up. He felt like the hand-me-down king of the universe. He tossed the tom-tom back into the closet.

Bean skipped music circle the next day. Ms. Halen-Hearty found him sitting on a stump. She guessed what was wrong.

"Bean," she said gently, "if I teach you how to make music without a fancy instrument, will you return to music circle?"

Bean was curious. "Okay," he said.

"Sometimes what we need is right in front of us," Ms. Halen-Hearty said. She showed Bean how to hold a blade of grass *just so*. When he blew on it, it made a wonderful sound.

Bean hurried back to music circle. Even though he didn't have the fanciest instrument in the group, he certainly had the loudest!

The next day was field day. Bean Bunny was hopping with excitement. He couldn't wait to run the hundred-meter dash.

"In your brother Billy's Ladidas sneakers, you'll be a shoo-in," his mother said proudly.

But Bean's hopes for winning the race were soon dashed. First, Kermit showed up in a pair of Lightning Heels. Then Piggy arrived in sneakers with a built-in pedometer. Rowlf had a pair of Bouncers. And Skeeter had on brand-new Treeboks.

How could Bean compete in a crummy old pair of hand-me-down Ladidas?

Bean sat on a bench and pulled on his old sneakers. *It just isn't fair,* he thought, tugging at his laces. Snap! The laces broke.

"Well," he said, "I guess I can't run." He walked off to go and sit on the stump again.

But Ms. Halen-Hearty followed Bean and sat down beside him. "Here," she said, pulling out a pair of shoelaces from her backpack.

Bean eyed the laces doubtfully. "It will take more than fancy laces to win," he said.

"That's right!" Ms. Halen-Hearty said. "It will take two fast feet. Remember, Bean—"

"I know, I know," Bean said, beginning to smile. "All I really need are the basics."

Bean relaced his sneakers and joined the others at the starting line. The camp director dropped the purple handkerchief—and they were off!

Kermit was in the lead until he looked down at his Lightning Heels and stumbled.

Piggy's pedometer wasn't working, so she sat down on the track to check it. Rowlf's Bouncers bounced him smack into Fozzie. And Skeeter got a new-sneaker blister and had to slow down to a limp. Bean Bunny won the race!

"Hooray!" cheered the other campers.

"What's your secret?" Kermit asked as everyone gathered around Bean.

"My two fast feet," Bean said, beaming. "And my hand-me-down Ladidas."

"They're cool," said Kermit. "Want to trade?"

"Nope," Bean said with a smile. "I wouldn't trade them for anything. Basics are the best."

# Let's Talk About Appreciation

Ms. Halen-Hearty taught Bean to appreciate what he had instead of wishing for something he didn't really need. In the end, Bean realized that hand-me-downs are just as good as new things.

Here are some questions about appreciation for you to think about:

Have you ever wanted something just because it was new? Did you really need it?

Have you ever been given a hand-me-down? What was it? How did you feel about owning it? What are some of the advantages of using things that aren't brand-new?